D0407847

The Sun and the Wind

Based on a story by Aesop
Retold by Mairi Mackinnon

Illustrated by
Francesca di Chiara

Reading Consultant: Alison Kelly
Roehampton University

"Look at me,"
said the sun.

3

"Listen to me,"
said the wind.

"I'm strong,"
said the sun.

"I'm stronger,"
said the wind.

8

9

"Show me!"
said the sun.

10

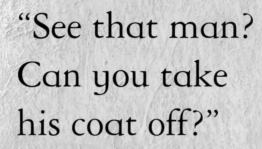

"See that man?
Can you take
his coat off?"

"All right,"
said the wind.

"He's hiding!
My turn," said the sun.

Look. He's coming out now.

17

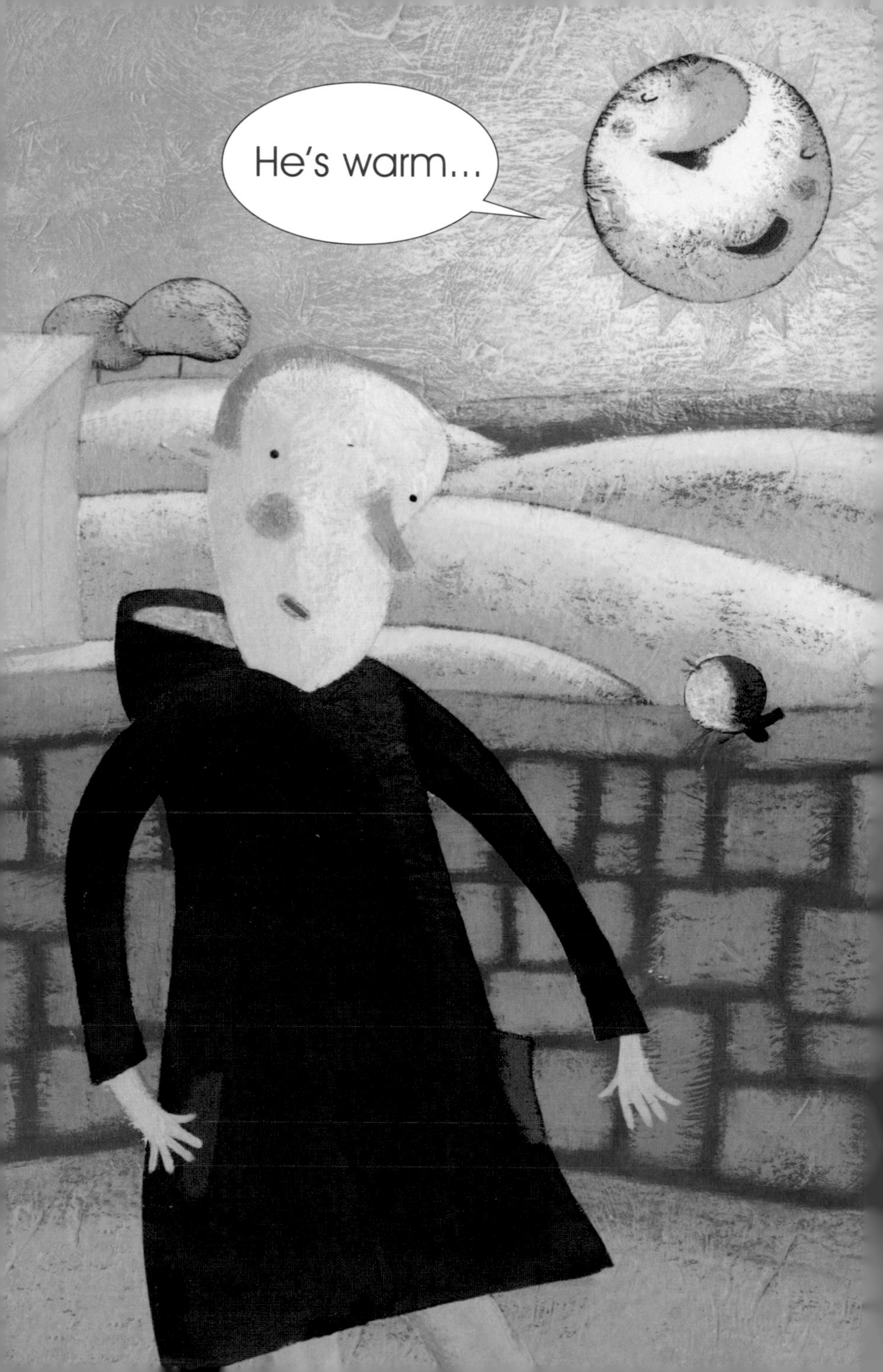
He's warm...

19

20

"I win," said
the sun.

"Huff!" said the wind.

PUZZLES

Puzzle 1

Can you see..?

a ball   a sandcastle   a dog

a cake   a bird   a blanket

Puzzle 2
What is the man doing?
Match the words to
the pictures.

B

A

eating   walking

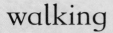

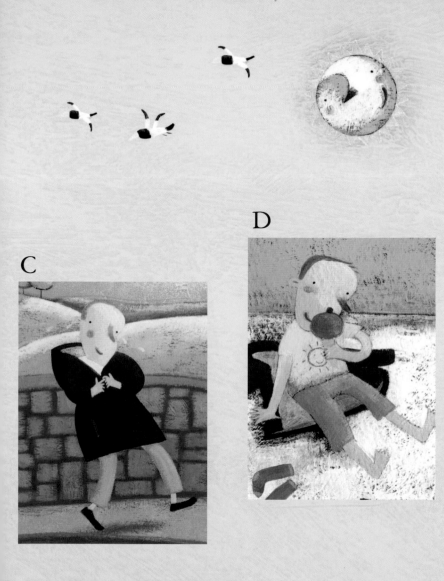

C

D

hiding   running

Puzzle 3

Can you spot the differences between the two pictures? There are 6 to find.

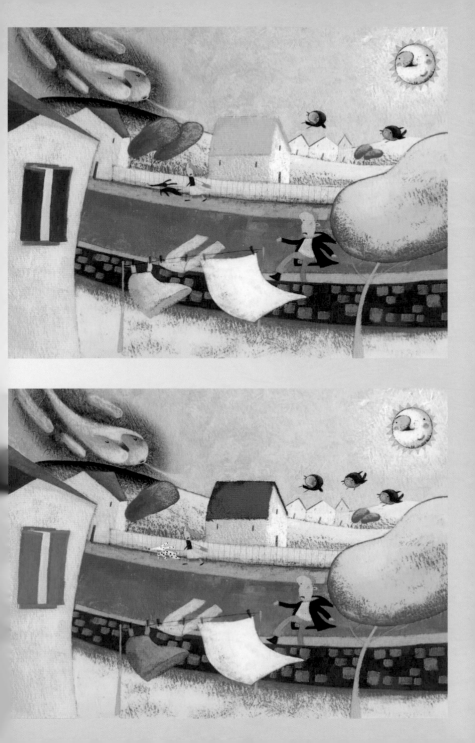

Answers to puzzles

Puzzle 1

a dog

a blanket

a bird

a cake

a ball

a sandcastle

Puzzle 2

A	B	C	D
running	hiding	walking	eating

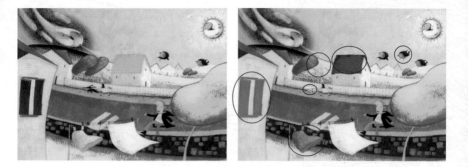

About the story

The Sun and the Wind is one of
Aesop's Fables, a collection of
stories first told in Ancient
Greece around 4,000 years
ago. Each story has a
"moral" (a message
or lesson) at the end.

Designed by Abigail Brown

Series editor: Lesley Sims

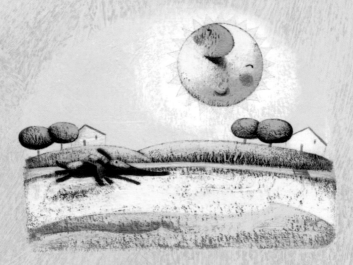

First published in 2007 by Usborne Publishing Ltd., Usborne House,
83-85 Saffron Hill, London EC1N 8RT, England. www.usborne.com
Copyright © 2007 Usborne Publishing Ltd.